THE STRANGER'S HOUSE

BOOK 1

OTIS BRIGHT

ISBN: 9798840569818

DEDICATION

This book is dedicated to my loving mom, Mrs Roseline Bright who supported my writing career right when I first started. She was my inspiration to keep letting my imaginations run wild and to keep writing and she's the main reason that this story was even possible.
This book is also dedicated to everyone else who has ever supported me in one way or another. I can list all their names but they know who they are. Thank you for all your support and this is for you.

CONTENTS

1.   PROLOGUE
2.   CHAPTER 1
3.   CHAPTER 2
4.   CHAPTER 3
5.   CHAPTER 4
6.   CHAPTER 5
7.   CHAPTER 6
8.   CHAPTER 7
9.   CHAPTER 8
10. CHAPTER 9
11. EPILOGUE

PROLOGUE

Greenly Bay, Wisconsin
October 1914

"Martin, my love, are you still there?" Elena Carey asked in a hushed tone as she lay on her deathbed, bleeding profusely with her stillborn baby cradled in her arms.

"I'm here, my dear, I'm right here," Martin answered.

He put a hand on the side of her head, assuring her of his presence. Her skin was so hot that he could feel it burning his palm but he bore the pain for he could not stand not being able to touch the woman he so loved.

"Why is our baby not crying, Martin? Why isn't it crying?" She asked in tears, fearing the answer she would get from her husband's lips.

"Our child…our child didn't make it. He didn't survive," He answered with a heavy heart, the pain overwhelming his senses as the words left his tongue.

Elena's heart broke after hearing him tell her the reason the child was so still, so quiet and she used all of her strength to lift the baby up to her face so she could see him.

"He's beautiful, Martin, just like his father," She sobbed when she saw her child's face.

"Yes, he is," Martin Carey knew his wife would soon join their baby in the afterlife and as much as he braced himself for the wave of pain that he would face, he knew he probably wouldn't be able to bear it. What was he to do without her charming smile that made his days brighter than the sun? How was he to dream again without her voice to inspire his creativity and spurn his desires? How would he ever laugh without hearing her jokes or sleep without feeling her arms around him? The answer was simple – *He wouldn't be able to do any of it.*

He was going to lose his only reason to be happy and it was because of THEM. Those filthy townspeople of Greenly Bay whose prejudices and small-mindedness blinded them to understand the reason for his and Elena's decision to use such "unholy" means to bear a child of their own.

When they found out the origin of her pregnancy, they slowly began to revolt but Martin never knew they would take it this far. They waited for the week when Elena would be due to birth the child and chose a time that would have been soaked and garnished with joy and turned it into a night of unfathomable loss for him and although they had taken his child and were soon to take his wife, they still wanted more and were banging on his door, demanding to get it.

"Give us her body so we can throw her in the river so her sins won't bring upon a curse to the town, Martin. What the both of you have done is blasphemous and will lead to nothing but chaos for this town if you do not surrender her corpse," One of the leaders of the mob screamed from outside his bolted doors as they tried to break it down.

"Do not let them have my body, Martin. Bury me and our child in the cemetery beside my parents' grave. Use the spell so they can never have my soul. Don't let them take my body and throw it into the water," Elena begged her husband, afraid for her soul which would never be able to rest if the townspeople got a hold of her body.

"I won't let them have you, my love, I promise I won't let them," Martin assured her although he wasn't sure how he'd keep them all away.

"Take my medallion and have it with you always," She removed the necklace from her neck with her bloody hands, "As long as you have it, I will always be with you and it will give you the power to fight against anything."

Martin took the necklace from her hand and when he felt it, it was colder than ice in his hand. Her magic was slowly fading away as the beats of her heart faded as well.

"You should also keep the book safe. You may need it later in the future. You cannot let them destroy it. It has all the spells, all the answers you'll ever need, everything," She told him.

"I have, my love. I've ripped out the page that has the spell to preserve your soul and I've buried the book where no one will ever find it," Martin assured her.

She smiled at him one last time, "Avenge me! Avenge our baby," The last words to come out of her mouth before her eyes shut forever and she drew her final breath, joining her baby in death with a slim chance for eternal peace.

Martin felt a piece of himself die with Elena and it was more pain than he had ever felt before. However, he didn't have time to mourn his loss because the door to his home was barely holding up and was about to be broken down by the angry townspeople. Martin needed to get Elena's and his baby's bodies away from them so he could bury them properly so they could find peace in the afterlife. He had to move fast because they got in.

He grabbed a sheet and wrapped his deceased family in it and carried them in his hands and made for the back door. He made his way outside and placed their bodies in the back of his automobile. At the same time, the townspeople finally broke his front door down and they stormed inside in their numbers to get their price.

"He's getting away," A woman screamed and pointed at the open back door.

They all ran outside but were too late as all they saw was the unsettled dust of the earth floating about restlessly behind the tire tracks of Martin's vehicle.

"We have to chase after him. The future of the town depends on it. Come on," The townspeople began to chase after Martin with their feet, desperate to get to him before he disposed of his wife's body.

Martin arrived at the cemetery and jumped out of his automobile. He grabbed a shovel that was lying around and began to dig as fast as he could because he knew if he could get Elena under the earth, the townspeople wouldn't be able to dig her out. He had put a great deal of distance between him and them so he had a few minutes to dig before they would catch up. The night was dark and the winds howled with the suspicion of rain as lightning streaked through the sky and the roaring boom of thunder echoed violently.

He dug the hole as deep as he could and when it was deep enough, he stopped. He went back to his vehicle and carried his wife's body and placed it inside the grave but before he could cover her up, one of the townsmen tackled him to the ground to make sure he couldn't.

"We won't let you curse this land," The man screamed and wrestled with Martin on the ground.

Martin grabbed the shovel and used it as a weapon. He managed to get the man off him but it counted for very little as the rest of the townspeople arrived as well.

He got off the ground and used the shovel as a

weapon to keep the people away from his wife's corpse.

"You know what we want, Martin. Let us take her and we won't have to hurt you too," The leader said to him.

"You cannot have her. You've already taken her child's life and hers as well. Isn't that enough? Have you no heart? The least you can do is let me bury her in peace," Martin cried out to them.

"She cannot be buried underneath the soil, Martin. Her crimes require punishment," The leader said.

"What other punishment can you inflict? You people are heartless, the lot of you! You stone a pregnant woman to death for what you consider a crime but what about your crimes?" He asked, his shovel still outstretched.

"That baby was an abomination and we could not allow his birth. It would have been the end of Greenly Bay,"

"That baby was a blessing and the lot of you stole him from me. I won't let you steal any more," Martin was ready to fight them all.

"Then, you leave us no choice. Get him out of the way and take the body," The leader instructed the others.

They all attacked Martin simultaneously and he swung his shovel, taking a few of them out but it wasn't enough. They surrounded him and were bringing him down when he grabbed the medallion Elena had given to him out of his pocket and held it out. The people saw the pendant and they all moved away from him in terror.

"The three-pointed star of the demon Moriah," A woman said before fainting out of fear.

"Stay back or I will unleash the power of this medallion on all of you," Martin threatened.

"I thought your wife was the only one who practiced witchcraft. I guess I was wrong," The leader said to Martin, "Burn him," He ordered the people.

They all threw their torches at him and he immediately caught on fire. He tried to put it out but they made sure he couldn't and watched him become engulfed in flames.

"Help me, help me, help me," Martin screeched in pain as the fire consumed him but the people just watched as he burned until he could remain on his feet no longer.

Martin collapsed and fell into the grave he had dug up for his wife, right beside her dead body. He looked at her face and shed a few more tears as his blackened body lay in the hole in the ground.

"Forgive me, my love. I couldn't keep my promise to bury you here but I will avenge you. From beyond the grave, from beyond death, from beyond the afterlife, I will make them all pay for what they have done to our family," He wrapped the medallion tightly in his grip.

The townspeople removed Elena's body from the grave and left Martin in it.

"What do we do about him?" Landon Willock

asked the leader.

He looked down at Martin's burned body and although he was still breathing, it was not enough to warrant saving him.

"He chose his path and now, he must suffer the consequences. We bury him alive. Grab the shovels, Landon!" The leader instructed.

Two of the townsmen, Landon Willock and Wilson Holmes, began to push the sand back into the grave while a few of them prayed to God for Martin's soul. As they covered him up, he swore to exact his revenge on them.

"You will all pay for this. Just as you have taken my child, I will take yours as well. I will take your children away from you and yours will be the first, Mathias Baker," He told the leader.

"You cannot harm anyone from the grave, Martin. May the good lord have mercy on your soul," Mathias said just as the sand covered Martin's dark eyes and enclosed him forever.

.

.

.

With Martin gone, the townspeople took his wife and child to throw them into the river as was their culture for women who practiced witchcraft; death by stoning and burial by water. Their town was free from any curse and their children did not die like Martin had threatened. The town felt that they had avoided a tragedy, unaware that they had only succeeded in delaying it for the time would come when a vengeful spirit will arise from the grave to carry out his promise of vengeance and return the favour; *an eye for multiple eyes, two lives for multiple lives and a child for hundreds of children.*

The heavens finally opened up and the rains descended downwards, covering the land with its cold and wet, turning the dirt into mud as the water got soaked into the soil, enriching the earth with its nourishment and life, a feat that the people took as a good omen; *rain after a witch's execution.*

They had no idea that the same water that nourished their lands would be the same to grow the seed that would sprout out from the ground and destroy their joy and kill their children. They had no idea about the power of a vengeful soul and the three pointed star medallion that was still wrapped in Martin's lifeless fingers. He would return, that much was a certainty. What wasn't certain was **WHEN.**

CHAPTER 1

Greenly Bay
October 14, 2018

Kevin rode across the street on his brand new skateboard with his friends who were riding theirs. It was a wonderful Friday afternoon and the boys were having fun, enjoying their holiday from school by skating freely.

They were very close to Kevin's house which was where they were headed to take a break from skating because they had been doing it all day.

"You guys want to see a new trick I learned?" Kevin asked his friends.

"Do it," Brandon, his best friend, told him.

Determined to impress his friends, an inexperienced Kevin picked up some more speed with his skateboard and tried the trick he had practiced but unfortunately, he wasn't able to stick it.

"Woah," Kevin exclaimed as he lost his balance and tumbled off his board. He fell on the side of the pavement and his skateboard wheeled over to the house opposite his and came to a stop on the lawn. "Kevin," Jamie, his other friend, called out and the two boys ran over to him, "You okay?" He asked. "Yeah, I'm fine," Kevin replied and got back on his feet, "I practiced that move. I don't know what happened."

"Maybe you need a little more practice," Jamie laughed at him playfully.

"Where's my skateboard?" Kevin looked around for it and spotted it on the lawn of the house, "Oh, there it is!"

He ran onto the lawn and grabbed his skateboard from the ground and when he raised his head, he saw a pair of dark eyes staring at him from the window.

Those eyes sent shivers down his fourteen-year-old spine and although he knew that it was their new neighbor staring at him, he felt like he was being stalked by a predator. All of his instincts told him to get out of there and he listened. "Sorry, sir," He said to the man before running off with his skateboard.

His friends ran behind him and they went into Kevin's house as quickly as they could.

"Who the hell was that?" Brandon asked.

"That was our new neighbor. He moved in a couple of days ago and he's really weird. All he does is just stare out of his window with those crazy eyes and it's so creepy," Kevin told him.

"Kevin, have you been bothering the new neighbor again?" His mother, the former Mrs. Jolene Baker said as she walked through the house looking for her yoga bag.

"No, I wasn't. I just went to get my skateboard from his lawn," Kevin replied.

"Good morning, Miss Jolene," Jamie and Brandon greeted at the same time.

"Morning, boys. Were you guys bothering the man?" She asked.

"No, we weren't," Kevin answered.

"Just make you stay away from him, okay. Some people just don't like to be bothered," She spotted her bag on the kitchen counter, "There it is,"

After grabbing her bag, she took out her car keys and was ready to head over to yoga studio for her class.

"Alright, I'm off and I'll be back in an hour," She rubbed Kevin's hair with her free hand, "Andy," She called out to her eldest daughter.

"What is it?" Andy replied broodily from upstairs and leaned out so her mom could see her.

"I'm going to the yoga studio and I'm going to need you to watch after your brother until your father comes to pick him up, okay?"

"Whatever," Andy replied and walked back to her room while texting on her phone.

"Make sure you keep an eye on him and not your phone, young lady," Miss Jolene screamed so she could hear.

"How am I even supposed to use this old thing? I need a new one but you refuse to get me one," Andy yelled back.

"It's okay, mom. I don't need her to watch me. I can take care of myself," Kevin told her.

"I know, baby. Be good at your dad's, alright?" She told him.

"I will," He replied.

"Great! I'll see you on Sunday evening."

Jolene walked out of the house and went into her car. She turned on the engine and drove out of the driveway and out into the street. That pair of dark eyes were watching her as she drove away and as soon as she was out of sight, they disappeared away from the window.

"And…she's gone!" Kevin said excitedly to his friends, "Let's go play some baseball outside."

"Yeah," His friends responded and ran outside while Kevin ran up to his room so he could get the ball, bats and gloves they needed for their game.

He burst his door open and ran into his room. He searched through his closet while making a lot of noise. Andy didn't like that he was so loud so she came out of her room and went over to his to make him stop.

"Why are you being so loud? I'm trying to talk to my friends," She yelled.

"Oh, cool it, I'm just trying to get my baseball gear so I can go play with my friends," He rolled his eyes at her.

"Shouldn't you be getting ready for when dad comes to pick you up?" She asked and folded her arms together.

"I'm already ready. My bags are packed and I have on clean clothes. As soon as he comes, we'll leave so please, go back to ignoring me."

"I'm already on that," Andy said and went back to her room.

Kevin found what he needed and took them back down to have some fun hitting his ball with his friends before his father would come for him.

"Ready?" Kevin asked Brandon who had the bat in his hands, ready to swing after the ball would be thrown.

"You know it," Brandon answered.

Kevin threw the ball and Brandon struck it with a powerful hit and it went soaring through the sky.

"Woah," Jamie exclaimed in awe and the boys watched the ball float through the air until it went over the fence and landed into the weird neighbour's backyard.

"Well, I guess that's the end of that," Kevin said because he was certain the ball was gone forever.

"Don't you have another one?" Brandon asked.

"No, that was my only ball. Let's just go do something else," Kevin said.

"What! No way, man. We just started the game and you want to quit because you're too scared to ask your neighbour for your ball back. Let's just go over there and ask him to let us into his backyard so we can get the ball," Brandon suggested.

"I don't know about that, dude. That man is really

weird. He freaks me out and I don't think it's such a good idea to be bothering him." Kevin replied.
"It's not a big deal. We'll just ask him and the worst that'll happen is that he'll say no," Brandon dropped the bat and began walking over to the man's house.
"You coming?" He asked his friends.
"Fine but you're the one who's gonna talk to him," Kevin ran to him but Jamie wasn't moving.
"Aren't you coming too?" Brandon asked him.
"Hey, he threw the ball and you hit it. I don't see why I have to come along," Jamie said smartly.
"You just don't want to come because you're scared. Coward!" Brandon said as he and Kevin went over to the neighbor's house.

The boys reached the man's porch and as they stepped on it, the old wooden deck creaked underneath their weight and it made Kevin tenser than he already was. They walked over to the front door and looked at each other to decide who would knock.
"This was your idea, bro," Kevin said.
Brandon rolled his eyes and pressed the doorbell but it didn't ring. He tried again but still, there was no sound. "Maybe it's broken. Try knocking," Kevin whispered.
Brandon raised his hands and just as he was about to knock on the door, it flew partially open and almost scared their ghosts out of them. The stranger was standing behind the door which was partly held open by the chain lock and he looked at them like they

were pests who were disturbing his peace and quiet.

"Umm, go-good, good day, sir. Umm, sorry to bother you but um, we were-we were playing on the other side and our ball got into your backyard and we were hoping, if it's not a bother that we could go get it?" Brandon asked nervously.

The stranger's eyes watched them intently and they never blinked, not even once. He shut the door close and they felt that he wasn't going to let them get their ball.

"Smooth. You sure convinced him," Kevin said sarcastically.

"I didn't hear you say anything," Brandon shot back.

"I told you this was a waste of time," The boys turned around to leave but stopped when they heard the sounds of the locks clicking behind the door, a lot of locks.

Finally, the door was unlocked and it slid open to reveal the stranger in full view. The kids braced themselves, expecting to see a gray-haired, bitter old man with crazy teeth, wrinkled skin and a bad attitude but were left surprised when they saw that he was a lot younger than they had envisioned. He looked like he was in his late thirties and his skin wasn't wrinkled at all. He was of average height and he had dark hair and all in all, he seemed like your normal everyday guy.

"Be quick about it," The Stranger said to them in a deep voice that was both terrifying and soothing at the same time. He moved aside for them to come in

and they looked at each other, silently asking themselves if it was a good idea to go in.
"Thanks a lot, Mr…?"
"Martin, Martin Carey," He answered.
"Come on," Brandon said to Kevin and they both went inside.
Martin turned around and led them to the backyard but he left his door wide open. After they went to the back, the door slowly closed on its own and the locks fashioned themselves in place.
They got to the backyard and Martin gestured at them to begin their search and as they did so, he watched them with hate and anger in his eyes which became red and they were focused slightly more on Kevin than they were on Brandon but whatever he intended to do, they were both going to suffer it.

****

"Wow! They actually got in," Jamie said to himself from Martin's house after he saw them go in.
He waited for almost ten minutes for his friends to come out with their ball but they didn't. He was getting a little worried but he just figured that they hadn't found it yet. He decided to go inside to get some juice while he waited for them to come back. He went into Kevin's house and walked into their kitchen. He opened the fridge, found the bottle juice, grabbed it and as he shut the fridge door, Andy was standing just behind it.
"Jesus, Andy, you scared the crap out of me," He

said nervously and almost dropped the bottle of juice.

"Where is the rest of your dweeb gang?" She asked.

"Why do you care?" He answered and grabbed a cup.

"I just want to make sure you guys are not doing anything crazy so my mom won't grill me about it when she gets back," Andy replied.

"They went over to your creepy neighbor's house to get our ball back," He responded.

"What? They went in?" Andy asked and she didn't sound happy to hear that.

"Yeah, they did and it's been quite a while and they haven't come out yet," Jamie said after taking a sip of juice.

"Ugh, I'm going to kill that Kevin. Come on, we're going over there," Andy said, grabbed Jamie's shirt and pulled him along.

They crossed the street and reached the stranger's porch and Andy knocked on the door but before she could get two knocks in, it slowly creaked open on its own and they were left with a choice; go in or stay out.

"Kevin? Brandon? You guys in here?" Andy called out but no one responded.

"What do we do?" Jamie asked her.

"We're going in there to find them. Come on," She said and took the first step in.

Jamie followed her and just as they made it past the door, it slammed shut and trapped them inside.

CHAPTER 2

"The door's stuck shut. It won't open," Jamie said while he struggled with the lock.

Andy knew something strange was going on and she could tell it wasn't good for them. She took out her phone so she could call her mom or the police or any adult that could get them out of this situation but she didn't have a single signal in her phone.

"What do we do, Andy? What do we do?" Jamie asked in a panic.

"I don't know," She said to him and she truly didn't, "Let's just find Kevin and Brandon and then we'll figure out a way to get out of here."

A subtle noise could be heard coming from somewhere in the house but they didn't know where it was coming from or what was making the sound. It sounded like static but it had an eerie feel to it which made the kids a lot more uncomfortable with being in this house.

"What is that noise?" Jamie asked Andy, his hand was now firmly gripping to hers and she didn't complain because she was also spooked out.

"I don't know but it sounds like it's coming from the living room," Andy said and took a step forward.

"What are you doing? We can't go in there," Jamie protested.

"Your friends are here somewhere and we have to find them. Stop being so scared and come on," Andy said to him.

She was trying to put on a brave act but she was just as terrified as he was. Everything about this house made her skin crawl; the creaky wooden floors, the plain white painted walls, the lack of any real lighting inside, the dusty cobwebs hanging from the ceiling, the weird smell it had, the deathly silence and most of all, that static sound was just too creepy and it caused her imagination to run wild.

They slowly walked through the house from the door and made their way to the living room to look for the boys. They got into the room and saw that the TV was on but it had no signal which was why the screen was white and that was what was making the sound they were hearing. There was also a rocking chair and a dormant fireplace in the corner which looked like it hadn't been used for decades.

"Hello, is anyone here?" Andy called out, "Kevin, where are you? If this is a joke, I'm telling you right now that it's not funny," She cried out.

"Maybe they're in the backyard. That's where the ball landed," Jamie said.

Andy decided to check the backyard and Jamie followed her very closely. They got to a sliding door that led into the backyard and went through it. There was no one there and it felt awfully chilly outside than it did inside.

Right in the middle of the yard was a white baseball, the same one the boys had hit into the yard. Andy slowly walked over to it and picked it from the ground and turned to face Jamie.

"Is this you guys' ball?"

"Yeah, that's it but, where are Kevin and Brandon?" Jamie asked and he was getting more scared with every second they were in there.

Suddenly, they could hear footsteps getting closer from just outside the street. It sounded like someone was passing by and that was exactly what they needed to get out of this predicament. Andy ran over to the fence which was too high to climb over. She began to hit against it, trying to draw the attention of whoever was passing by.

"Hello, is anyone out there? Please, help us, please," She cried out just as the person was passing by.

She looked through the slabs of wood and could see the outside. She saw that the person passing by was their other neighbor, Mrs Gail so she called out to her.

"Mrs Gail, thank God it's you. Please, you have to help us. We're trapped in her and I think the new neighbor is a kidnaper or something li-" Andy said to the woman but she just walked by like she didn't hear anything.

"Mrs Gail? Mrs Gail, can't you hear me? Mrs Gail, please come back! Mrs Gail," Andy screamed after her while slapping the fence but nothing she did seemed to be getting the woman's attention because she didn't even look over there and was now gone.

Andy stopped screaming out to her and turned around to look at Jamie and they were both now certain that something weird was going on and it wasn't good for them at all.

"She couldn't hear me. She didn't hear," Andy told Jamie.

"So, if we can't call for help with your phone and no one can hear us, how do we get out of here?" Jamie asked.

"I don't know…but before we think about that, we have to find my brother," Andy said.

They walked back to the sliding door and went back into the house. A few things weren't the way they were expecting to find them when they got back inside. For one, the TV wasn't on anymore, that weird smell was gone and was now replaced with what smelled like smoke and if Andy wasn't mistaken, burning flesh.

The kids decided to search in some other part of the house for Kevin and Brandon so they walked into the kitchen but it was empty.

"Where are they?" Jamie asked in frustration.

Unbeknown to them, someone was coming up from behind them. The figure was right behind Andy and was just about to grab her shoulders when she turned around.

"Maybe they're upstairs," Andy said to Jamie, unaware that someone or something had almost grabbed her just a second ago.

The two of them walked out of the kitchen and went over to the foot of the stairs and stopped to just stare at the staircase before going up. They didn't have to say anything to each other because it was obvious what the other person was thinking. Going up was a completely different ballgame and they needed to be sure that it was the right, safe, or sensible thing to do.

"Are we really going to go up there?" Jamie asked.

"They could be up there and they could need our help. We have to go," Andy replied.

She decided to let go of her fear and climb up those stairs and find her brother. She took a deep breath and raised her leg to put one foot on the first step.

"Don't go up there!"

Kevin jumped out of nowhere and grabbed Andy's hand to stop her from going up the stairs.

"Jesus!" Jamie screamed in shock and fell to the floor in fear.

"Kevin, we've been looking all over for you and Brandon. What is going on here and is that blood on your face?" Andy hugged him before examining his head for injuries.

"I'm fine. It's not my blood," Kevin said and pulled her hands away.

"If it's not yours, then whose is it?" Andy asked but Kevin stayed silent.

"Kevin, where's Brandon?" Jamie asked.

"He took him," Kevin replied.

"Who took him? Who took Brandon?"

"The Stranger," Kevin said with fear in his eyes and tremor in his voice.

Right outside, just opposite the stranger's house, a car pulled into the driveway of the Bakers and a tall handsome gentleman stepped out of it with a stuffed teddy bear and a brand new phone in his hands. He walked over to the front door and rang the doorbell. He waited a while but no one came out to receive him so he decided to knock on the door instead.

He did so and waited a few more seconds but still, no answer.

"Kids? You in here?" The man called out.

He decided to open the door and he walked inside and checked all over the house to see if he could find anyone.

"Kev? Andy? You guys in here?" He called out but quickly realized that there was no one in the house but him.

He went back out and went to the backyard to check for them but he couldn't find them. He felt like something was wrong so he decided to call their mother to ask about where their children were.

Jolene was in her yoga studio speaking to some of her friends while they waited for the instructor to show up. She could hear her phone ringing in her bag so she excused herself and went to check it.

She took the phone out of her bag and saw that

the caller ID was Joe, her ex-husband and she sighed before answering.

"Hello, Joseph. I take it you're calling to let me know that you just picked up Kevin," She answered.

"Well, I'm here at the house but the kids are not here," Joseph told her.

"What do you mean the kids aren't there?" Jolene asked, confused.

"I mean, they're not here as in, the house is empty. I can't find Kevin or Andy anywhere,"

"Well, have you checked their rooms or maybe the backyard?" Jolene asked.

"Jo, I've checked everywhere. I've looked upstairs, the garage, the attic, I've even asked some of your neighbors but no one knows where they are. They are gone, Jo," Joseph told her.

Now Jolene was starting to panic. She was starting to realize that something was wrong with her kids and her heart began to beat a lot faster as her fear and maternal instincts began to kick in.

"If they aren't at home, then where are they?" She asked, already almost in tears.

Back inside the stranger's house, Kevin was telling Andy and Jamie about what was going on and he sounded demented because some of the stuff he was saying wasn't making any sense.

"Kevin, slow down and explain to us what's going on here," Andy said to him in a calm voice.

"This place is haunted, Andy and he's-he's

watching us. He's watching us and he's going to kill us, he'll, he'll kill us all," Kevin said nervously, stuttering on every word.

"Is Brandon okay, Kevin?" Jamie asked.

"I don't know. I haven't seen him in days and I've just been trying to survive…"

"Hold on, Kevin. What do you mean by days? You've been in here for maybe like thirty minutes," Andy told him.

"What? No, that can be! I mean I don't have a watch, but it's been at least two days since Brandon and I came in here," Kevin said, completely in shock by what his sister was telling him.

Suddenly, a loud bang echoed all around the house and Kevin looked so terrified. He could sense that HE was coming and he knew what it meant for them.

"We have to hide! We have to hide now, we can't let him find us. Come on, quickly," Kevin urged them and ran over to a broom closet.

Andy and Jamie followed him and when they got to the closet, Kevin shoved the both of them inside before going in himself. It was dark in the closet so Andy used her phone to give them some light.

"Kevin, what is happening?" Jamie asked.

"Shush," Kevin told his friend, "Keep quiet, both of you. Don't say a single word…and don't move at all until I tell you to."

"But-"

"Until I tell you to, Andy," He said again.

The kids all became quiet and they could hear

some loud footsteps coming from outside the door. The person that was moving sounded like a giant because of how loud his steps were. There was also a clicking sound when he moved and with every clink, Kevin flinched every single time he heard it.

He was peeping outside the door of the broom closet and could see the man's shadow. He looked at his friend and his sister and gestured at them to stay quiet.

"Oh, Kevin! I know you're down here and I know you have company. Come out and I promise you, I'll make it slow and painless unlike how it played out with little Brandon," The stranger said from outside.

His voice felt like ice and it was filled with sorrow and hate, like a broken man in search of something to make him whole but at the cost of the safety of others. He was demented and his goal was clear and nothing was going to stop him from carrying it out. Absolutely nothing!

CHAPTER 3

"There's no point in hiding, kids. I will find you and you will pay for what they did to my wife," The Stranger said from outside.

Kevin had his finger out to Andy and Jamie, urging them to remain silent while they waited for the Stranger to walk by them. If they remained silent long enough, then they would be able to survive even longer.

"I made a promise and I intend to keep it," He said again as he moved around.

His footsteps suddenly couldn't be heard anymore and it seemed like he was gone, for now. Kevin waited for about a minute before he decided to check. He slowly opened the door of the closet and looked outside. The Stranger wasn't there and all that remained of him were a few muddy footprints that trailed off into the darkness before disappearing out of sight. Kevin sighed in relief before going back inside to tell them that they were safe for now until he showed up again.

"He's gone. We can talk now," Kevin said.

Andy turned the light of her phone back on and

they continued talking about what was happening to them here.

"Who is that man and what is he talking about? Why does he want to hurt us?" Jamie asked.

"I don't know who he is or why he's after us. All I know is that he wants to kill us and we can't get out of here," Kevin said, still sounding unhinged due to the torment of being in here for so long with survival being the only thing on his mind.

"What happened to you, Kevin? What has happened to Brandon since you guys came in here?" Andy asked, wanting more explanations from him.

"Everything seemed normal when we first came to his doorstep. He introduced himself, said his name was Martin Carey, and he let us in to find our ball. We went to his backyard and we started looking for it, and then…" Kevin paused.

"And then what?" Andy asked.

"Everywhere got dark as if it was about to rain and the lawn caught on fire and the flames drew a weird shape on it. It looked like a star with three points and as soon as I saw it, I felt something change within me. I felt a piece of myself die and that's when I knew we shouldn't have come in here," Kevin said as he recalled what had happened from his perspective.

In the Baker's home, Jolene had returned from the yoga studio because of how worried she was when Joseph told her that the kids weren't anywhere to be found. They had also called the police and two officers had driven over to their house to speak to them about their missing kids.

"You have to find my children, officers. Please, you have to find them," Jolene begged the policemen.

"I understand how you feel, ma'am, but we can't have officers running around town looking for your kids when they've only been gone an hour," One of the officers told her.

"You said your daughter's seventeen and your boy's fourteen, right?" The other officer inquired.

"Yes," Jolene answered.

"And your boy had two of his friends over before you left and they are also nowhere to be found?" He asked again.

"Yes, but what does that have to do with them being missing?" Joseph asked him.

"Well, when a group of kids disappear for this long, it's rarely ever a kidnapping or anything like that because those kinds of crimes usually happen with just one kid or maybe two but never four and never at this time of day. You know how kids their age tend to sneak out to parties and they run off all the time, especially in homes like yours where a particular parental figure isn't always present," The officer said.

Joseph and Jolene were offended by the officer's comment because he was insinuating that they weren't doing a good job of raising their children.

"Now, listen here officer! Our kids aren't

rebellious just because their father and I are divorced. They are old enough to understand the situation and they would never just run off. My daughter's phone isn't going through and that has never happened before. I'm telling you that something isn't right with my children and you have to find them now," Jolene raised her voice at the officer.

The officers could see that Miss Jolene was very distressed by the situation so they did what they could to ease her worries.

"Okay, this is what we can do for you at this time. We can send a patrol car to drive around town and keep an eye out for your kids but until it's a complete twenty-four hours that they're gone, we can't treat their absence like a missing person's case," The first officer told her.

"So, what do we do?" Joseph asked.

"Well, one of you can search around town and look for the kids anywhere you think they could have gone while one of you stays here in case they come back. You should also keep in touch with the other kids' parents in case they hear anything and if the kids don't show up, then we will do everything we can to find them," The second officer said as he and his partner turned around to leave.

"But they could be in trouble," Jolene shouted to the officers and Joseph had to hold her back to calm her down.

"No need to panic so much, ma'am. I'm sure they'll turn up any minute now. Have a good day,"

The officers walked out the house, got into their car and drove away.

"What do we do, Joseph? What do we do?" Jolene asked him, scared for her kids' safety.

"We just have to calm down, Jo. Maybe the officers are right. Maybe the kids just went somewhere and are probably on their way back. I'm going to drive around town and look for them while you stay in case they come home," Joseph said calmly and wiped the tears from the side of her face.

"Do you remember the places that they go to?" Jolene asked since he hadn't been living with them for a few years now.

"Of course I remember. It hasn't been that long since you kicked me out of my own house, you know," He said jokingly to try to get her to laugh.

She let herself smile a little before sending him off to find their children. He went outside and she followed behind him. He got in his car and looked at her for a few seconds before starting the engine and driving away.

Jolene was alone now and she looked around the street, hoping to see Andy and Kevin walking towards home but they weren't. Her eyes fell on the house just across the street opposite hers, the house of the Stranger but she turned away from it and went back inside, unaware that her children were in there and they were fighting to stay alive.

.

.

.

"What the hell is that?" Brandon asked as he crawled away from the fire on the ground.

I was on the other side of the lawn and I moved away from the fire as well. The flames made the shape of a three-pointed star and it slowly began to rise out of the ground. The wind that was blowing in the backyard was very intense and we could hear it howling like ghosts in the wind. The fire grew larger until it was out of the ground. It began to shape up into what looked like a demon but judging from some of its outlines, it was a woman. The fire woman was making ghostly sounds as she waved around in the wind. She turned her head and faced Brandon. He swallowed in fear and crawled away from her but there was nowhere to go. She spun around and looked at me as well before opening her mouth to speak.

"An eye for multiple eyes, two lives for multiple lives and a child for hundreds of children,"

The woman in the fire cackled like a witch and the winds blew stronger than before. She laughed hysterically before she began to swirl around, slowly getting sucked back into the ground until she disappeared completely and the wind ceased.

"Mr Martin? What was that?" I said but then I noticed that Mr Martin was gone.

"Where did he go?" I asked Brandon.

"Who cares where he went? Let's get out of this mad house," Brandon yelled at me and the two of us got on our feet and ran out the sliding door and headed straight for the main door. We got to the door but couldn't open it because the multiple locks around it were fastened and they just wouldn't come undone. We tried to break the door down by kicking it several times but it was no use, so we started screaming for someone to help us. Brandon and I could see Jamie sitting outside on our porch and we called out to him but it didn't seem like he could hear us.

"Why isn't he coming over here?" Brandon asked me, scared and panicked just as I was.

"He isn't coming because he cannot hear you. No one can hear you inside this house and no one ever will,"

We heard a strange voice say those words but when we turned to see who was speaking, there was no one there. The voice sounded like Mr Martin but in many ways, it didn't. It sounded more like someone who was angry and wanted to take out that anger on us.

"Who said that?" I asked Brandon and he looked at me with oblivion in his eyes because just like me, he didn't know what was happening.

It became deafeningly quiet inside the house. There wasn't any sound at all, not even a whisper of wind, and it felt like the space in front of us was expanding and it scared Brandon and I so badly that we could barely stay on our feet. Something was watching us and it wanted to hurt us.

The floor creaked underneath my feet and when I

stared down to see what made it creak, a wet muddy hand burst out of the floorboards and grabbed my foot and just like that, I felt my soul leave my body as the fear came in to replace it. The hand felt so cold and its grip was so strong it felt like my foot was getting ripped off my leg.

"Brandon, help," I screamed for assistance and he grabbed my hand and struggled to pull me away from the hand.

A second hand came out of the boards and grabbed my other foot and was slowly pulling me down into the hole. I was so terrified. I didn't want to die.

"Brandon, please do something," I cried to him.

He began to stomp on the hands with his feet. He clamped on the fingers several times and we could hear them snap like fallen twigs from a tree in autumn. The hands finally let go of me and I crawled over to Brandon, shaking in terror. The hands went back into the ground and for a moment, we thought it was over…but it wasn't.

They burst out again, much more powerful this time and we could see quite clearly that someone was trying to get out of the ground and the ghoulish sound he made was unlike I had ever heard.

"Come on, let's move," Brandon shouted at me and we both ran as fast as our legs could carry us. We ran up the stairs as quickly as we could and made our way into a room and closed the door. We thought we were safe but when we turned around, we saw them all over the walls, nailed on there like decorative ornaments, the most surreal thing our young innocent eyes had ever seen.

"Are those what I think they are?" Brandon asked me as we both trembled at the horrific sight.

"Yes it is. Skeletons of other kids," I swallowed as I said it. I could tell the bones weren't adult bones because of the sizes and it made me feel as though I was about to be hung on that wall.

CHAPTER 4

"What happened next? Andy asked him.

"Before we could even react, a hook attached to a chain burst through the bedroom door and caught Brandon right in the shoulder. He screamed and his blood got all over me. The Stranger pulled him outside, dragging him through the wooden door. I held onto his legs and tried to keep him from being dragged away into the darkness but my hands were slipping and I just couldn't hold on to him. I let go and Brandon's screams were the last thing I heard before it became silent again," Kevin said.

Jamie was teary-eyed, believing that his friend was dead now and that they were next.

"I ran down the stairs and since then, I've just been trying to survive. I never thought I'd see either of you again," Kevin said with a little bit of gladness.

"Do you know if Brandon is still alive?" Andy asked.

"I don't! The Stranger claims to have killed him

and now, he wants to kill us as well. We have to find a way out of this place, Andy. We have to."

"We will get out of here, guys, I know we will. Our parents must be looking everywhere for us and it's only a matter of time before they realize that we're here and they're going to come and save us. We just have to hang on for as long as we can," Andy said.

The flashlight on Andy's phone suddenly started to malfunction. It went out for about a second before she tapped the scream and it came back on and went out again.

"Come on, not now, you old phone," She said to the device while tapping it.

"Do you really think our parents will find us soon?" Jamie asked.

"Of course, they will," Andy replied and the light came on again.

As the closet lit up again, there were four heads inside of it, not three.

"No, they won't," The Stranger said and the kids screamed in terror before bursting out of the closet and running for their lives.

As they ran, Andy tripped on a mat and fell to the floor as the Stranger came out of the closet and approached her. He had his hook in his hand and for the first time since she arrived at the house, she could see him clearly and completely.

He was wearing a dark old suit but from what she could tell, it was burned in some places. His eyes were bloodshot and his skin didn't look fresh. He was like a walking talking corpse and just the mere sight of him made her too petrified to even stand up and run for her life. Despite him being covered with mud from head to toe, Andy noticed the medallion around his neck and saw that it had a star on it, a star with three points and for just a moment of looking at it, she saw a woman's face and could feel the sadness in her deep blue eyes.

"Time to die, Baker," The Stranger said just as he raised his hook, preparing to bury it into her.

Kevin ran over to his sister and pulled her away just in time to avoid the hook that crashed right where her head was and into the floorboards.

"Come on, Andy," Kevin helped her up, "Let's move! Up the stairs, now," He shouted and the three of them all ran up.

"That's right. Run as fast as you can but in the end, it won't matter how fast you run. You'll all die eventually, just as my little boy did," The Stranger said and pulled his hook out of the floor.

The kids all ran up and Kevin was in front of them leading the way. He moved through the corridor and gestured at them to follow him. They ran past a series of doors and when they made it to the end of the corridor, Kevin didn't know what to do next.

"Where do we go, Kevin?" Andy asked him.

"I don't know. I've only ever been in three rooms since I got here. The closet downstairs, the bone room and..," He paused, almost like he couldn't get the words out of his mouth, "...another room,"

"Well, we have to do something," Andy went to a door and was about to open it.

"Wait! We don't know where this door could lead. This house isn't normal and we could be walking into a trap," Kevin tried to be cautious.

They could hear the wooden stairs creaking as the footsteps of the Stranger echoed against them. He was heading up the stairs and was coming for them. They needed to decide.

"If we stay here, he'll catch us and kill us. This is the only option we have," Andy told him.

The Stranger's head was visible now. He was at the top of the stairs and he turned his head towards their direction.

"For the love of God, just open the door," Jamie shouted. He panicked and pushed Andy out of the way so he could open the door.

He twisted the nob and opened the door. They all ran inside the room and the door shut on its own after they were inside.

They suddenly found themselves falling through a dark empty space and they all screamed in fear, not knowing what they were falling into. They eventually hit the ground and as much as it hurt, they didn't sustain any serious injuries. Kevin grunted on the ground and slowly got back to his feet. He ran over to Andy and helped her up and then, he went to Jamie and helped him up as well.

"Are you guys okay?" He asked them and they both nodded affirmatively.

"What is this place?" Jamie asked.

They all looked around and surveyed where they were and by the looks of their surroundings, it didn't seem like they were inside a house anymore. They were outside, on a piece of land and it was dark and foggy so they couldn't see quite clearly. After Jamie backed into a huge stone and tripped, the others ran to him and helped him up. They looked at what he had tripped over and saw that it was a tombstone.

The fog suddenly cleared away and they could see a lot clearer now where they were. They were at a cemetery, surrounded by the graves of thousands of dead people, with no way out and no one else around but them.

"I don't like this place," Jamie said and clung on to Andy in fear.

"Why would that door lead us here?" Andy asked, her question directed at her brother.

"I don't know. Maybe it brought us here for a reason. Maybe there's something here that can help us better understand what's going on and why that man is trying to kill us," Kevin answered.

"So, should we like, look around?" Andy asked.

"It's all we can do, Andy,"

The kids began to look around for anything that could explain their situation. They had to be brave to move around those graves and they were. They searched around for anything they could find. Andy looked at the tombstones with her flashlight and was reading the names etched on them in her head until she came across one that had to mean something.

"Kevin, come take a look at this," She called out to him. He and Jamie walked over to her and stared at the stone she was pointing at.

"Look at the name written on this one," She told him.

Kevin leaned over and read the name out loud, "Mathias John Baker…That's the name of our great-grandfather," He said to her.

"That's right," Andy replied.

"Why are we at our great-grandfather's grave? What does he have to do with any of this?" Kevin asked.

"He's not the only one here," Jamie said from the very next grave.

Andy and Kevin went over to him and saw the stone he was looking at and it had his last name on it as well, "Landon Willock! That's the name of my great-grandfather," Jamie said.

Kevin took Andy's phone and used the light to look at the next grave and just as he suspected, it had Brandon's family name written on it as well.

"Wilson Holmes! That's Brandon's great-grandfather," Kevin told Andy.

Kevin looked around some more and the last names on a lot of the graves were familiar to him. They were the names of his friends at school, friends whose families had lived in Greenly Bay for generations and all of their ancestors were buried here, in the same cemetery. It had to be connected somehow, he thought.

"These are all the graves of our predecessors here

in town. Every single one of them. But why?" Kevin asked.

While Kevin and Andy wondered what was going on, Jamie turned around and noticed another grave, separated from the others and the stone on it was a lot bigger as well. There was something about that grave and Jamie felt like he needed to get a closer look at it. He moved away from the others and slowly approached the grave. When he got about a foot away from it, he read what was written on the stone silently.

"Kevin, the man who lives in this house; what did you say his name was again?" Jamie asked.

Andy and Kevin walked over to the grave and saw what was written on it and it became more apparent that the person they were trying to survive from, was a ghost.

"Here lies the discarded body of Martin Carey. Practitioner of the dark arts and traitor of purity. His and his wife's evil actions almost brought a curse upon our land but the brave men and women of Greenly Bay made sure it didn't."

Kevin read the inscription on the stone and from there on, they were able to start putting several pieces of the mystery together.

"So, what does this mean? Martin Carey was killed by our great-grandparents and now, his spirit wants to get revenge by killing the descendants of the people who killed him?" Andy wondered.

"That seems to be the case but the question that we need to be asking now is; why? Why did they kill

Martin Carey? What was this evil action that he and his wife committed that made the people kill him?" Kevin asked.

While Jamie and Kevin stroked their chins and scratched their heads, trying to figure out the reason, Andy stared at the tombstone of Martin's grave and saw that same symbol on it; the same three-pointed star symbol that she saw on the medallion around the Stranger's neck.

Just like the first time, she fell into a trance-like state and as she looked upon the star, she saw that same face again, the woman's face clenched in pain as she tried to push out her baby. Andy could feel her heat, her stress, her sadness and her joy when the baby finally got out of her.

"Why isn't our baby crying, Martin? Why isn't it crying?" Andy heard the woman ask and the words were like stones in her heart.

"Andy?" Kevin shook her back to reality, "Are you okay?"

She blinked for a few seconds, trying to recompose herself and after she did, she looked at Kevin and then at Jamie, "They had a baby,"

"What are you talking about?" Jamie asked.

Suddenly, a bony hand burst out of the grave of Mathias Baker and the same thing started to happen to all the graves of the dead townspeople. The kids screamed in fright as they witnessed the corpses rise from their graves one after the other.

"We have to get out of here," Jamie screamed and started to run.

Kevin and Andy were behind him and behind them was a group of skeletons chasing after them. A hand burst out of the soil and grabbed Jamie's foot. He fell down and with terror in his eyes, he tried to free himself from the hand but he couldn't.

"Guys, help…" He called out to Andy and Kevin who just made it to him.

Kevin grabbed a rock and smashed the hand apart, freeing Jamie. They continued running until they saw another door just standing in the corner of the cemetery but there was no wall around it.

"Come on," Kevin urged them and when they made it in front of the door, he opened it.

They couldn't tell where this door would lead or what was inside of it but, just like the first time, they didn't have that much of a choice. They all went in and the door slammed shut after they went inside.

CHAPTER 5

As the kids entered through the door, they found themselves in a place that felt like it was an actual room in the house because there were walls around them with several pieces of furniture sitting around.

Andy still had her flashlight on because the room was lit up by a lone candle on the table in front of them. It was more of an altar than it was a table and everything about the room just had a spooky feel to it; it felt occupied by something or someone.

"Where are we now?" Jamie asked.

"Only one way to find out," Kevin said and began to move towards the candlelight.

The closer they moved toward the light, the louder the floorboards creaked. The room was all dark except for that light and they could already tell that there were other things on the altar apart from just the candle. They reached the altar and Andy went ahead to survey all the things that were on it.

There was a lot of dust and cobwebs all over the

altar which meant that no one had been in this room for a long time. There were also a few other items which included, two daggers with some foreign words carved against the side of the blades, an old book with a picture of the three-pointed star on the cover, a picture frame of a beautiful woman, and a sealed envelope.

Andy picked the picture and wiped the dusty frame with her hand so she could have a better look at it. When she saw the woman's face, she realized that it was the same face she'd been seeing whenever she looked upon that star; the face of the sad woman giving birth.

"I've seen this woman before," Andy said to the boys.

"Where?" Jamie asked.

"I've just been—like, having visions of her and I also heard her voice. I think she was the wife of Martin Carey,"

Kevin's eyes spotted the daggers and he grabbed them from the altar. He kept one for himself and gave the other to Jamie who didn't understand why he was being armed so he hesitated to collect it.

"We need to be able to protect ourselves when he comes again. Take it," Kevin told him and he took the dagger.

"What else is in this room?" Kevin asked.

Andy put the picture frame back and went for the envelope next. She broke the seal and took out the note that was inside. She unfolded it and saw that it was a letter.

"It's a letter written by Martin Carey and it's addressed to a woman named Elena Carey. That must be his wife," Andy said and began to read it:

```
My dear Elena,
     Ever      since     I      returned,
everything   has    been    completely
different   without   you.   I    still
don't  know  how  I  can  exist  in  a
world  where  you  are  no more and it
fills   my   heart   with   sadness   to
know    that    we    could    never    be
reunited again, not even in death.
Know  that  I  love  you  and  that  I
love   our   son   and   know   that   no
matter  how  long  it  takes,  I  will
avenge   you.  One   by  one,   I   will
take  away  their  children  as  they
did ours. I will not rest until I
kill   every   single   last   one   of
them.  They  will  suffer  just  as  I
have  and  their  spirits  will  never
find   rest   knowing   that   it   was
their   actions   that   damned   their
generations  to  the  cutting  edge  of
my wrath.
     Though   you   aren't   able   to
rest because of what they did with
your  body,  my  dear  Elena,  take
solace   in   knowing   that   none   of
them will be spared. As the power
```

of the medallion fills my rage, as the kiss of the demon Moriah fuels my hook and as the desire for vengeance lights my way, know that I will carry on your final request for as long as my body walks upon this wretched land.

Greenly Bay will suffer and none of them will survive. They will all pay. This I swear to you, my love!

October 1985

"Woah! That was intense," Kevin said.

"So, what's the story here? Our great-grandparents killed his wife and child and now, he wants revenge by killing us?" Jamie asked, standing closest to the door.

"Something's not adding up," Andy said and looked at the letter again.

She looked at the timestamp on this letter and saw that it said October 1985 and it got her thinking.

"When we were in the cemetery, on Martin's gravestone, the day he was killed was written on it. It was October 1914 but the date on this letter is October 1985, and that can only mean one thing…"

"He rose up from the grave," Kevin said.

"So, we're being pursued by a vengeful ghost?" Jamie asked, facing his friends.

"That's right, Little Jamie,"

The light bulbs on the ceiling suddenly came on and the Stranger was standing right behind Jamie. He thrust his large hook into Jamie's back and the hook burst right through his chest, with his heart attached to it and still beating.

"Jamie, no…" Kevin screamed as his friend's blood splattered all over him and Andy.

The Stranger lifted Jamie into the air and the boy could be heard choking on his own blood. Kevin was angry and scared. He clenched the dagger around his hand and for a second, thought about attacking the Stranger but Andy grabbed his hand and pulled him away.

"C'mon, let's get out of here," She screamed and dragged him towards the door.

"But, Jamie..,"

"We can't save him, Kev," She said and dragged him along.

They ran out of the room and were in the corridor upstairs. They quickly went down the stairs and when they made it down, Kevin stopped and stared up, waiting to see what would happen because he could hear some footsteps slowly approaching the top of the stairs.

"Kevin, we have to run," Andy said to him.

"Wait, wait," He told her and watched.

The footsteps got louder and the Stranger's shadow could be seen from the corner getting bigger as he got closer but then, it stopped and everywhere was even more silent than the grave.

"Why is he just standing there?" Kevin asked and

he got his answer almost immediately.

From up the stairs, Jamie's body was thrown downstairs and it landed on the floor, right in front of Andy and Kevin. He was dead and his heart had been ripped out of his body. Kevin slowly approached his friend's dead body while Andy looked away in horror, unable to stare at the horrific sight.

Kevin began to sob as he looked down on his friend's corpse, his mind was in a rut and he couldn't think clearly or even get a word out of his mouth.

"Kev, we need to move," Andy said, also in tears.

The same hook that was used to kill Jamie also got thrown downstairs and fell down the stairs until it came to a stop beside Andy's foot. The siblings looked up again and saw the Stranger standing at the top of the stairs with a chainsaw in his hands.

"Which one of you is next?" He asked and turned the chainsaw on and began heading down the stairs.

Mourning time was over and the kids needed to run for their lives yet again.

"Let's go, Kev," Andy said and helped him up and they ran to the other side of the house where they hadn't been yet since they got here.

"It doesn't matter how much you run, kids. You're both still going to die. There is no escape from your fate," the Stranger taunted as he descended.

He faced the direction that the kids had run and just as he took a step forward to go after them, he heard the doorbell ring just from behind him.

"Hello, is anyone here?" Jolene called out from outside the house.

The Stranger faced the door and began to approach it with his chainsaw still in his hand. He got to the door and reached out one hand to open it. He turned the knob and opened the door about halfway.

"Hi, there! Um, good afternoon sir," Jolene greeted the man.

"Good afternoon. Can I help you?" Martin asked her.

He wasn't in his burnt muddy suit and neither did he have his chainsaw with him. His skin looked like that of a normal person and Jolene saw him as just another neighbour she could ask for information concerning her kids' whereabouts.

"I don't mean to disturb you or anything, Mr…"

"Martin, Martin Carey," He answered

"Mr Martin…I don't know if you're aware but my kids have gone missing. I realize that we don't know you that well but since your house is right opposite ours, I was wondering if you happened to see anything strange this afternoon over at my house by any chance," Jolene asked desperately.

"I'm sorry, Miss…"

"Jolene," She said.

"Jolene…but I didn't see anything. I haven't even been outside the entire day," Martin said.

Jolene looked like she was about to cry and she couldn't hold it in anymore.

"I'm just so worried about them," She burst into tears, "I've been asking around the neighbourhood but no one has seen them and now, I don't know what to do,"

"I'm sorry about that. I can relate with how you must be feeling because I've lost a child before," Martin said dryly.

"You have?" Jolene asked.

"Yes, I have. It's a terrible thing when a parent loses their child. It happened to me and I didn't ever get the chance to be with my boy again but I'm sure you'll be with your children soon enough."

While Martin spoke to Miss Jolene at the door, Andy and Kevin were in another closet, hiding from him and they had no idea that their mother was right at the door. Andy still had her phone flashlight and when she moved it around, she realized that it wasn't a closet that they were in; it was an indoor toolshed.

"Kevin, look…" She said to him, "There's stuff in here that we could use to fight against him,"

She gave her phone to her brother and started picking out the most dangerous and lethal tools she could find while Kevin just sat on the floor, shivering because he was still very much disturbed by what had happened to Jamie. That image was still stuck in his mind and he couldn't get it out.

As Andy searched through the shed, she stopped when she heard some voices coming from outside the room. It sounded like two people having a conversation and she wondered where it was coming from.

"Do you hear that, Kevin?" she asked her brother and he tried to listen as well.

They could hear a woman's voice speaking to a man and they realized that it was coming from just down the hall. More than that, Kevin recognized the woman's voice.

"That sounds like Mom," He said.

Andy's eyes widened in realization and a smile unconsciously crept onto her face, "It **Is** Mom," She cried out and ran to the door.

She turned the knob and opened it and saw that Martin Carey was standing at his door, speaking to someone who was surely their mother.

"Mom..." Andy was about to call out to her when the door of the toolshed suddenly slammed shut on its own.

"No, no, no, Mom help," She screamed and tried to open the door but it was stuck shut and wouldn't open.

"Mom, we're in here," Kevin joined her to scream and they were both hitting the door, desperately trying to get their mom to realize that they were in there but she couldn't hear them.

"Well, I hope they come home soon," Martin said to Jolene.

"Me too," She answered and turned around to leave.

Martin watched her walk away with an angry glare. He looked back into the house and could hear the children screaming for their mother from somewhere within and he growled in annoyance. He closed the front door and his entire self slowly transformed into his true form; the muddy dead man with a chainsaw in his hand.

He began to walk in the direction of the sound of the screaming and the banging. He didn't turn the chainsaw on so the kids wouldn't hear him coming.

CHAPTER 6

The Stranger was at the door of the shed and could still hear the screaming and banging coming from inside. He smiled, pleased by their desperation to survive, to live, the same one his wife and baby had. They were strong enough to try to cling on to life even after being pelted with rocks but it just wasn't enough to get them over the line.

He sharply opened the door and after he did, a hammer flew at him and hit him right in the eye and got stuck in it. Kevin and Andy were breathing heavily and they thought that they had hurt him a little.

"You know, it's going to take more than a hammer to stop me," He pulled the hammer out of his eye and threw it away. He brought his chainsaw forward and smiled at the children before turning it on.

"Now, who's next?"

Andy and Kevin kept throwing tools at him in

fear but he was just laughing at them and he took a step closer with the revving saw and the siblings screamed and held each other for what was to come.

"Hey! Stay away from my friends, you son of a bitch," Brandon screamed at the Stranger, pointing the barrel of a shotgun at his head.

"There you are,"

"Yeah, here I am," Brandon replied and pulled the trigger and let a round into the Stranger's head.

He stumbled back but was still on his feet so Brandon loaded another round and shot him again. The Stranger was out of the doorway now and was dazed and confused so the kids were able to come out of the shed.

"Oh my God, Brandon, you're alive," Kevin said when he saw him.

"No time for that. We need to move," Brandon said and shot at Martin yet again, blasting him to the floor.

"Come on! Follow me," Brandon told them and led them back up the stairs.

Andy and Kevin stopped when they saw that Brandon was trying to take them back up again and they really didn't want to go back.

"What's the matter with you guys? Come on, he's not going to be down for long," Brandon yelled at them.

"We just came down from there," Andy told him.

"There's a room up there where we'll be safe from him and he won't be able to find us. That's where I've been this entire time and he wasn't able to get to me," Brandon said and gestured at them to come along.

Andy and Kevin didn't have a choice but to go with him. If there was indeed somewhere in the house that the Stranger wouldn't be able to get to them, then that's where they needed to be.

They were on the top corridor and Brandon ran around looking for a particular door but he didn't seem to remember which it was.

"Brandon, I saw him hook you up and drag you away. How are you still alive?" Kevin asked him.

"I guess I got a strong will to live," Brandon answered and found the door he was looking for, "Alright, this is it."

He opened the door and they all went inside and just like every door in the haunted house, it closed on its own.

That door led them to the edge of a river and it was late at night and there was a full moon shining in the sky. Brandon walked over to a tree trunk by the river and sat down on it. He dropped his shotgun by his side and massaged his left shoulder with his right hand.

"Come on, guys. Come sit," He said.

Kevin walked over and sat down on the ground beside Brandon while Andy sat on a branch opposite the both of them.

"So, Andy was the one who came in here looking for us and not Jamie? That kid is so scared of everything but I guess in this case, he was right to be afraid and not come," Brandon said jokingly and laughed a little.

He looked at Andy's expression and also at Kevin's and he could tell what they were thinking.

"He did come, didn't he? And now, he's not with you guys and…" He sniffled and rubbed his eyes, "He's dead, isn't he?"

Neither Andy nor Kevin replied and that was all the confirmation he needed to know that it was true. He wanted to cry but he held in his tears, refusing to show any weakness because of what he had to survive so far against the Stranger.

"At least, we'll be safe here for a while," Brandon said.

"What is this place anyway?" Andy asked.

"I don't know but for some reason, the Stranger can't follow us in here. Well, he can but he won't get this close to the water. It's almost like he's afraid of it or something," He replied.

"How did you survive, Brandon? I saw him hook you on the shoulder. I saw him pull you into the darkness. I heard your screams and then, I heard nothing," Kevin asked his friend.

"I thought I was good as dead but I guess I had more desire to live than I thought," Brandon said and began to narrate what happened to him from his perspective.

After I felt his hook stab into my shoulder, I thought for sure that that was it. I felt him tug and I was sliding down the floor and when Kevin grabbed me, I had a little bit of hope that I would make it but unfortunately, Kevin wasn't strong enough to hold on.

The Stranger pulled me and I was transported into this graveyard. There were graves all over the place and I was so scared and so hurt. The Stranger dragged me toward an empty grave and when I saw it, I realized what he wanted to do to me; he wanted to bury me alive.

"Don't worry, Little Brandon. It will all be over soon," He said to me with that spine-cracking voice.

"No, please, don't do it," I begged him but he didn't care.

The closer I got pulled to that grave, the more fear I felt. I don't know what it was that just took hold of me. Maybe it was my fear, or adrenaline, or maybe it was just plain old determination but it took hold of me and gave me the strength I needed to save myself. I grabbed the hook on my shoulder and I pulled with all of my strength until I ripped it out of me.

I immediately got on my feet and I turned around and faced him. I stared into those red eyes and all I saw in them was pure evil. Those weren't the eyes of a person, no. Those were the eyes of a demon, a soulless demon.

"I see you have a lot of spirit in you," The Stranger said to me and pulled the chain of his hook back into his hands, ***"I'm going to enjoy draining it all out of you,"***

He started walking toward me again and my instincts kicked in and I just ran. I didn't know where I was going or if there even was a way out. I just ran as fast as I could and he chased after me. He would swing his hook at me and each time, he missed very narrowly. I was running out of breath and I was just so tired and just when I was about to give up, I saw a door and it was just standing there so I ran over to it.

I opened it and I ran inside and the next I knew, I was back in the house, right where he had taken me from but Kevin was gone. I called out to him but he never answered. I entered another room and I rummaged through the things that were in there, looking for something to defend myself with and that's when I found this beauty hanging on the wall but unfortunately, there weren't any bullets in it. I also found some flares, a little can of gasoline, and a matchbox so I grabbed them as well.

I ran to the door and just as I opened it and came, that hook came at my face but I ducked underneath it. I crawled under his legs and he grabbed my foot so I slipped out of my shoe and ran into this door.

"Run as much as you want but there is no escape from me, Brandon,"

He followed me into the door and I ran through

the woods and he just kept coming, relentlessly trying to catch me. That's when I made it to the edge of the river. Since I can't swim, it dawned on me that I was trapped and he was right there, ready to hook me up again. I fell and I crawled closer to the water and as soon as my hands made contact with the water, the Stranger just stopped moving toward me. Those evil eyes suddenly had some emotion in them and it was sadness and fear.

"No, not the river...Not the river," He whimpered and just like that, he ran back the way he came.

I realized that there was something about the river that he didn't like and so, it became my safe space. I've been going back into the house, gathering bullets, some more flares, supplies and any other weapons that I could find and whenever he came after me, I would just run back in here and he wouldn't follow.

"So, he's afraid of water?" Andy said.

"I think it's just this particular water, this river. Maybe something bad happened to him here or something," Brandon said.

The kids now had a little bit of an advantage against Martin Carey but they still didn't have a way out of here and they knew that they wouldn't be able to stay by the river bank forever. They needed a way out.

"Have you found anything that can help us get the hell out of here?" Andy asked.

"No, I haven't. This house has a lot of doors but unfortunately, none of them is an exit back into the real world," Brandon said.

"Well, we need to find something that can give us more information," Kevin said, "Something like those writings on the tombstones or that letter or—"

"This book," Andy said and took the book out of her shirt.

"You took the book?" Kevin asked.

"What book?" Brandon asked as well.

"It's a book we found in one of the rooms. We didn't get a chance to read it because the Stranger attacked," Andy said.

"It has that same symbol on it; the star with three points. I've seen that symbol all over this house. There must be some good information in there," Brandon said.

Andy unhooked the cover of the book and opened it. She flipped through the pages but she couldn't understand what was written on it because it wasn't in English.

"This is like Latin or something. I don't understand it," She moaned in frustration.

Brandon took the book from her and stared at it but he too didn't understand the words written on it. The pictures however, were easier to translate.

"Does this look familiar to you guys?" Brandon asked and showed them the page with a medallion drawn on it.

"The Stranger's Medallion," Andy whispered and snatched the book back from him.

She flipped through the pages quickly and saw images that look familiar to her. She saw an image of a man crawling out of a grave, covered in mud, "This looks like Martin's empty grave and this man is covered in mud, just like he is," She said to the boys.

She scanned through the book some more and saw another image of a woman giving birth to a baby with horns, "I had this weird vision or something where I saw a woman giving birth and it looked a lot like this," She said again and kept scrolling.

"Guys, this is a spell book," Kevin said.

"You're right Kevin. Everything in here is a spell," Andy said.

"And if it has information on how to cast spells, it should have information on how to break spells as well. We need to be able to read this book," Brandon said.

"I have an app on my phone. It can help us translate the book," Andy said excitedly and took her phone out of her pocket.

"But there's no internet service here. The app won't work," Kevin said.

"No, it will. It's an offline app," Andy took out her phone and when pushed the power button, she gasped.

"What is it?" Brandon wondered.

"I only have three percent battery left. It won't be enough to go through the entire book,"

And for that moment, the hope they thought they had slowly dwindled away and the fear returned to replace it.

CHAPTER 7

"Okay, turn the next page," Andy said to Kevin and he did.

She took a picture of the next page and waited for about thirty seconds for the app to translate it. After it was translated, Andy quickly read through it and muttered inaudibly as she did.

"Does it say anything about escaping a haunted house?" Brandon asked her impatiently.

Andy didn't respond to his question. She just kept reading the page and after she was done, she nodded negatively to the both of them.

"Alright, next page," Kevin said and they continued in that manner.

Andy's battery was now two percent and they still had a lot of pages left to translate. It wasn't looking like they were going to make it.

"Next one," Andy said again.

Kevin turned the next page and a picture of the two daggers they had found on that altar was drawn on it. Andy took a picture of the text and after it got translated, she skimmed through it and read that it was a powerful weapon that was thousands of years old and that it could kill demons on earth.

"This isn't it either. There's nothing about escaping a house here. Next page," Andy told Kevin and he flipped again.

"This is hopeless," Brandon complained, "We're never going to find what we need before her phone dies out. We don't even know for sure if there's anything written in there that could help us escape this house,"

"Well, we're not giving up," Andy said and read another page but after she was done, she didn't have any good news for them.

They translated another page and that was also not the spell they were looking for. Things got even worse when she showed them the screen of her phone and they saw that there was only one percent battery left.

"Damn it," Brandon cursed out.

The kids all slumped to the damp ground and they seemed like they were about to give up hope that their salvation could lie in the spell book. Kevin placed the book on the ground and covered his face with his hands while Andy stared at her phone like it was a traitor that was leaving her in her most desperate time.

"What do we do now?" Brandon asked.

"I don't know," Andy replied.

She slowly reached for the book and slowly

flipped the pages. She flipped through page after page and that was when she began to notice a similar pattern in the book. For every heading of a spell, there was a picture attached to it; a picture of what the spell should look like. This was what they should have been doing all along.

"Guys, check this out!" Andy screamed in excitement, placed the book back on the ground, and knelt over it.

"What? What is it?" Kevin wondered.

"The pictures are a clue to what the spells are," She said as she flipped the pages, "We just have to find a particular page that has the picture of kids looking like they're trapped or in trouble,"

"Or," Brandon stopped her from flipping and went back two pages, "a page with a picture of a scary house," He pointed out at the picture in the book.

"This could be it. This could be our way out of here," Kevin said with a smile.

Andy took a picture with her almost-dead phone and it loaded in the app for what felt like an eternity because of how anxious the kids were.

"Why is it taking so long?" Brandon screamed in frustration.

Finally, the picture was done loading and the transcribed text appeared on the screen.

"There, it's done," Kevin said.

"THE ENTRAPMENT SPELL, cast to trap the bodies of your enemies in an inescapable prison so that you

may hunt their souls to quench the thirst of your anger and vengeance," Andy read from the book.

"Yeah, that sounds about right. This is definitely it. Keep reading," Brandon urged her.

"The spell is initiated after the caster summons the presence of the demon MOR-I-AH, whose dark, powerful and ancient magic possesses a wide space and makes it an inescapable loop of portals into the heart and soul of the caster, displaying their grief and pain while their undead soul seeks to destroy their trapped victims,"

"We don't need any of this information. Look for any part that talks about how to break the spell," Brandon said and Andy did as he said because she knew he was right. They didn't have the time to read the whole thing.

Andy flipped to the next slide of the app and saw the word 'break'.

"This should be it," She said and continued reading;

"To end the spell and free the entrapped, the medallion of Moriah would have to be destroyed and..."

Andy's phone suddenly went dark as the power gave out completely before she was able to finish the sentence.

"No, no, no," She screamed desperately and tried

to turn the phone back on but it was completely out and refused to come back on.

"Was that it?" Kevin asked, hoping she would say yes.

"There were a few lines left that I wasn't able to read," Andy said.

"But the book said to destroy the medallion to break the curse, right?" Brandon asked.

"Yes, but what about the rest of it? What if we didn't get all the information we needed?" Andy asked.

"This is all we've got, guys. It's our only chance so we know what we have to do. We've got to get that medallion and destroy it and hope that it works. It's our only play here, guys."

Both Andy and Kevin knew that Brandon was right. They didn't have any other option than to destroy the medallion and hope for the best.

"Alright, but we still have a problem. How are we supposed to get that medallion off Martin's neck without being ripped in half by him?" Andy asked.

"We're going to have to load up," Brandon said with a smile.

"What do you mean load up? And why do you have that look on your face?" Kevin asked.

"You'll see. Come on!" Brandon said and got on his feet, "Andy, grab the matches and the can of gasoline. We'll need a lot of things that can cause some damage,"

Andy grabbed the gas can and the matchbox as well. Brandon started walking away and the siblings followed behind him, wondering where he was taking them.

He walked out of the woods and led them back to the door that would take them back into the house.

"Where are we going, Brandon?" Andy asked.

"When I found this gun, I was in a rush to get away from the Stranger but I'm pretty certain that this wasn't the only gun in that room. If we can get back there and get you guys some guns of your own, then maybe we'll have a better chance at getting that medallion," Brandon said.

Andy and Kevin looked at each other and nodded in agreement. They were going to stick with Brandon's plan.

"Alright then, let's do this," Brandon pushed the door open and the kids all ran out through it.

.

.

.

At the Bakers' home, Jolene was still waiting outside for her children's return and her eyes were reddened from all the crying that she had been doing. It was getting late and the sun was preparing to set and still, no word from them. She couldn't take it anymore. She couldn't just sit there and do nothing when Kevin and Andy were still not home. She had to do something more than just wait for them so, she got to her feet and was about to comb the entire town until she found them.

That was when Joseph's car pulled up by the edge of the sidewalk and immediately Jolene saw him, she ran over to his car, hoping he brought the children along. His windows were tinted so she couldn't see into the car as she approached it but she was praying to God that they were in there.

Joseph opened the car and got out. He faced Jolene and when she saw the look in his eyes, she realized that he wasn't able to find them.

"I'm sorry, Jo. I've looked everywhere but I couldn't find them," Joseph told her.

"What? How can that be? Where could they have gone, Joseph? We have to find them. I know—I can feel it in my heart that they're not okay," Jolene cried and wasn't even sure what to do at this point. It was getting too much for her to bear.

"I'm certain that they're fine, Jo..." Joseph said and tried to hold her but she pushed him away.

"No, you're not!" She raised her voice at him, "You don't know anything for certain. We have to call the police and get them to look for our kids," Jolene cried, holding her head with both hands.

"The police won't do much unless it's been twenty-four hours since the kids are gone," Joseph reminded her.

"I don't care what they say. If we haven't been able to reach our children for this long, it means they're in trouble. Why won't the cops understand that? Why won't they..." Jolene broke down and Joseph wrapped his hands around her, comforting her with a hug and trying to get her to calm down.

"We'll find them, Jo. We'll find them, you'll see," He said while shushing her softly and patting the back of her head.

"I never should have left them all alone. This is all my fault," She cried.

"No, it's not your fault Jo," He said to her while looking her in the eye, "You can't blame yourself for this. It's not anyone's fault and we will find them,"

He resumed his hug and tried to put on a brave face for her but the truth was that he was even more terrified than she was. He needed to be strong for her but deep down inside, his heart was breaking and he wanted nothing more than for their children to just show up.

....

Brandon was ahead of them and he had the gun raised in case the Stranger would attack. He also had some two flares attached to his trousers and a knife in his left shoe. Kevin was armed with the dagger he found on the altar while Andy just had the spell book.

They quietly moved through the top and he led them into the room where he had found his gun. Once they got in, they discovered that the room was completely dark but after they all made it past the door, the lights on the walls all flickered on and made the space bright. Brandon was shocked to see that the room was now completely empty.

"Where have you brought us, Brandon?" Kevin asked because there was nothing in here.

"I—I don't understand. There was a big closet right there and there was also some furniture over there and the guns, the guns were in this corner and, and..," Brandon became confused.

"He knew we were coming here," Andy said softly and she seemed worried, "It's a trap," She spoke out louder.

The door of the large empty room suddenly slammed shut and the lights went out and everywhere became dark again.

"Stay together, guys," Brandon shouted and they all scrambled together, unable to see each other.

Brandon took out one flare and pulled the top off and the red light from it made it better for them to see what had made its way into the empty room with them. The Stranger was standing right in front of them and Brandon threw the flare on the floor and raised his gun.

"I've had enough of these games," He said and fired the motor of his chainsaw.

"Brandon quick, shoot him," Andy yelled.

Brandon fired the shot gun but Martin moved like lightning and was able to get out of the way, avoiding the pellets. He shot again and Martin dodged again while getting closer to them. Brandon screamed like a madman and kept firing until Martin was right in front of him.

He raised his chainsaw down on Brandon who raised the gun and used it as a shield. The saw was quickly cutting through the barrel of the gun and out of fear and desperation, Kevin jumped in to help Brandon.

"Get away from my friend," He screamed and stabbed the Stranger in the stomach with the dagger.

"Argh," Martin grunted and slapped Kevin away from him and he crashed into Andy. Brandon also backed away to where his friends were and the Stranger loomed over them.

He was ready to finish them off but his red eyes widened when he realized what had just happened. For a split second, he looked scared and then, he just…disappeared.

The lights in the room came back on after he was gone and the kids were so relieved that he was gone. They were also confused and didn't understand why he just left when he could have easily killed them.

"Did you see the look on his face before he fled?" Kevin asked, "It was almost like was afraid,"

"I think he was," Andy said and the boys turned to her, "He was afraid of the spell book. I think he saw it in my hands and ran away in fear of it,"

"…because he knows that we know how to kill him,"

Brandon   added.

CHAPTER 8

Since the kids couldn't find any more weapons, they decided to go after the Stranger with the weapons that they had. They just had to stay together and get that medallion off his neck so they could destroy it and break the spell. Brandon had his shotgun, Kevin had his dagger and Andy only had a little can of gas and some matchsticks in her pocket. They weren't exactly well-armed but they didn't have that much of a choice but to go and fight for their freedom.

"Guys, stay close," Brandon told them as they moved down the stairs.

They walked down the creaky staircases until they made it downstairs. The kids could hear the sound of something creaking from the living room and they walked over to check on it. After they got to the living room, they saw that the TV was on again and just like when Andy and Jamie first arrived, it didn't have any signal. The fireplace that had been dormant before now had some logs burning in it which made the room warmer and brighter. The rocking chair was also in front of the TV and someone was sitting on it, rocking back and forth which was where the creaking sound was coming from.

They slowly approached the person and Brandon raised his shotgun, ready to shoot.

"It wasn't supposed to be like this, you know," Martin said from the chair.

They could see that he was in the same form that they first found him when they first arrived at his house to get their ball. He wasn't muddy, his eyes weren't red, he was wearing a robe instead of his burnt suit and he wasn't holding any weapons. The Stranger was gone and all that was left was Martin Carey.

"We were a normal couple and all we wanted was a child to make our happiness complete but no matter how hard we tried, we just couldn't conceive…"

"We don't care about what happened hundreds of years before we were born. We just want to get out of here so give us the medallion or we will take it from you. We have the spell book and we know how to kill you so you'd better let us out right now," Brandon said aggressively, trying to sound intimidating.

"Elena's family had some history with witchcraft, it ran in the blood of their family and their practices had been passed down to every woman in her family for generations," Martin kept talking, ignoring Brandon's threats, ***"She***

suggested that we try a new approach to have a child by seeking help from a demon. At first, I was skeptical about the idea but I loved her and I knew that it would make her very happy so I agreed. She took the medallion and prepared a spell to summon the demon,"

The television suddenly went dark for a few seconds before coming on again and this time, it now had a signal and there was a moving picture on it; some of Martin's happiest and saddest memories that were being played for the kids to see.

.

.

.

On the TV, Martin could be seen drawing a three-pointed star symbol around his wife who was sitting with her legs crossed in the middle of their bedroom. She had the medallion in her hands and the spell book was placed on the floor right in front of her.

Martin completed the drawing and looked at his wife so she could tell him what to do next.

"Light three candles and place them on the end of each point," Elena instructed.

Martin did as she said and she asked him to stay back while she summoned the demon.

"Are you sure this is going to work, Elena?" Martin asked because he was worried and was having second thoughts.

"It will work. The demon will give us what we desire. I have witnessed this spell with my own eyes when I was a little girl. My grandmother performed it for a friend and she was able to finally have a child. It will work, my love," Elena replied with certainty, "No matter what starts to happen to me, do not touch me or the spell will break. Do you understand me, Martin? Do not touch me," She warned.

"I understand but what will happen to you?" He asked.

"You'll see," She said.

Elena flipped through the pages of the spell book until she got to the page of the spell that would summon the demon, Moriah. She closed her eyes and began to read out the incantations, asking the demon to show herself and bless her womb with a child.

"O magnum daemonium! Tuam in me industriam invoco, et potentiam tuam invoco. Benedic me puero ex utero tuo. O Moriah, reple me vita nova, o Moriah," She read the spell in Latin, summoning the demon and asking her to fill her womb with a living child.

A powerful gust of wind blew into their bedroom but the candles didn't go out, they even burned brighter. Elena's eyes rolled to the back of her head, showing only the whites and Martin looked on with worry. She started vibrating and she was snatched into the air by an invisible entity and shook her around the room. She was being shaken violently through the air and occasionally got slammed into the side of the walls.

Martin could see that she was being hurt by the demon she was invoking and he wanted to go and help her but he remembered her warnings and although he hated doing nothing, which was exactly what he did. After a while, Elena became frozen in the air and she had blood dripping from the bruises she had sustained from being slammed around by the power of Moriah. She had her eyes closed and it didn't seem like she was conscious.

"Elena?" Martin called out to her as she remained frozen and suspended in the air.

"Elena?" He called again.

Her belly began to rise and grow, getting fatter and fatter until she was full and lumpy. She was slowly lowered onto the bed and placed gently on the mattress. After she touched the fabric, another gust of wind blew and this time, it blew the candles out and flipped all the pages of the spell book until it was closed shut.

Martin slowly approached Elena on the bed and when he got to her, he saw that she was pregnant and it was even far along. Elena opened her eyes and the first thing she noticed was the size of her belly.

"It worked!" She whispered happily and a tear escaped her eye, "She's given us a child, Martin,"

Elena put her hands out, inviting her husband into her embrace. They were so excited and grateful that their dreams were finally being realized.

"We're going to be parents," Martin said and kissed her lips with so much joy.

"Yes, we are," She replied and they were so happy.

.

.

"It felt like a beautiful dream and I never wanted to wake up from it ever. I was going to have my family and I was happy," Martin said again to the kids.

"How many times do I have to tell you that we don't care about any of this?" Brandon screamed.

"Brandon, stop!" Andy yelled at him, "Let him finish,"

"But why do we have…"

"Just let him finish, man," Kevin said to him also and he grumbled angrily.

The TV came back on and the series of events that happened after the conception played out on the screen for the kids to see.

About a week after the conception of her baby, Elena began to notice that the townspeople of Greenly Bay all whispered to themselves about her whenever she came outside. Some whispered while some said their minds aloud for her to hear.

They all felt that her pregnancy was unusual because she wasn't pregnant just a week ago and now, she was so heavily pregnant. Rumors spread that her baby was the spawn of the Devil himself and anytime Elena went to the markets to buy things, none of the traders would agree to sell to her. At first, Elena was bothered by the people's behavior but later, she stopped caring what they said or how they felt. The most important thing to her wasn't her status in the society, it was the birth of her baby.

"When will the baby be due?" Martin asked her while they were sitting in their living room one evening.

"I'm not exactly certain but it should happen in about a week," Elena said.

"What do you think it's going to be? A boy or a girl," He asked her.

""I don't really have a preference. All I know is that I'm going to love this baby with every fiber of my being. I'll be the best mom to it," Elena said.

"And I'll be the best dad," Martin said and kissed her belly.

"Well, the best dad has to go to Hickson's store to get the provisions we need," Elena said with a smile.

"I thought you said you were going to go there today?" Martin asked.

"I did but the women refused to sell to me. They still hate me and it's gotten even worse now," Elena said.

"They don't hate you, my love. People just tend to fear what they don't understand," He kissed her forehead and stood up, "You hang tight! I'm going to run over there and got what we need,"

He grabbed his coat and walked out the door. When he got outside, he could smell that it was soon going to rain so he began to run to the town's store, unaware that when he would return, it would be to a mob that had pelted his pregnant wife with rocks.

.

"I was gone for only twenty minutes and on my way back, I could see the bright light from people's torches shining in the distance. I reached my house and I saw my wife lying on our porch, bleeding and near death. I forced my way through the crowds and went to her. I couldn't believe what they had done to her and I desperately carried her inside and locked our door to make sure they wouldn't follow,"

The TV played out the gruesome scene for the kids to witness. They saw how the townspeople had surrounded the house after Martin left and how they began to throw things at the house. They saw how Elena came outside to beg them to stop what they were doing and how they ruthlessly attacked her by hurling huge rocks at her. It was not a pleasant scene to watch.

"I couldn't save my wife or my baby. I lost them that night because of your ancestors and like that was not enough, they killed me as well. Buried me alive like I was nothing. People claim to hate evil acts but are willing to commit them in the name of 'doing the right thing' or righting a wrong. It's hypocritical, wouldn't you agree?"

Martin asked and spun the rocking chair around to face the kids just after the TV shut itself.

"Listen, Mr Martin, what happened to your wife and child was a terrible crime and I am sorry about that but we aren't to blame. You have to let us go. Your wife would not want you to be doing this," Kevin said to him.

"Yes, she would. Getting revenge was her idea after all," Martin said just as his eyes became red.

He instantly became covered in mud and his robe transformed into his burnt suit just as the rest of him transformed into The Stranger. His chainsaw appeared from out of nowhere and he launched out of the rocking chair and headed for the kids.

"Move!" Brandon pushed Kevin out of the way and blasted The Stranger with a shot from the gun.

He staggered back but remained on his feet. He raised his head and his active chainsaw and ran at Brandon. The kid fired the shotgun again but the Stranger ducked underneath it and brought his chainsaw down on Brandon who raised the shotgun across his body as a shield to prevent him from being ripped apart by the rolling blades.

"Argh," Brandon screamed, fighting with all his strength to keep the blades away from his body and the Stranger was pressing down hard, trying to cut him up.

Kevin ran over to them and held the handle of the chainsaw, trying to pull it away from Brandon. While the three of them struggled with the saw, Andy put down the gas can, ran over to the rocking chair and grabbed it. She carried over to where they were and slammed it against the Stranger's back in an attempt to get him to leave the boys alone. This seemed to anger him and he used his palm to slap her across the face and she landed beside the fireplace.

That swift movement he made opened him up and Brandon saw the medallion tucked inside his suit around his neck.

"Kevin, grab the medallion," He screamed.

Kevin saw the necklace around his neck and reached for it. He grabbed it and the Stranger had no choice but to let go of the chainsaw so he could stop Kevin from getting the medallion.

After he dropped the chainsaw and grabbed Kevin's hand, Brandon raised the shotgun and blasted the Stranger right in his face and sent himself, the Stranger and Kevin crashing into the floor due to a small explosion from the gun's pellets after they hit Martin, which caused the medallion to rip off his neck and fall to the floor.

"Brandon, there it is," Kevin pointed at the cursed item.

He cracked his shotgun and fired a shot at the medallion which ripped it apart and destroyed it completely.

"Nooooooo," The Stranger screamed and crawled over to the destroyed necklace and held its pieces in his hands, ***"What have you done? What have you done?"*** He yelled frantically.

CHAPTER 9

"What have you done, boy?" The Stranger yelled again.

Just as he asked the question, the door that led to the outside blasted open and the kids' freedom was only a few steps away.

"We did it!" Brandon said in elation, "Let's get the hell out of here,"

He was the first to make for the open door and just as he was to reach it, the Stranger made sure he didn't.

"You're not going anywhere, boy," He raised his hand and the floorboards turned to dust and broke apart underneath Brandon's weight.

He sunk into the floor of the house and was trapped in there from his legs to his waist. Brandon struggled to get free but he couldn't pull himself out.

Kevin and Andy were down and the former had sprained his ankle after the small explosion so he couldn't get up quickly when he saw that the

Stranger had his eyes set on Brandon.

The Stranger got off the floor and picked up the chainsaw yet again. He quickly walked over to Brandon while starting the saw up again and when he reached him, he brought the rotating blades of the saw down on Brandon's head.

"No, Brandon!" Kevin screamed but his screams were drowned out by the sound of the chainsaw drilling into Brandon's skull and his blood splattered everywhere.

The Stranger kept the saw on his head and increased the power until he was able to slice past his head and down into the rest of his body and tore him in half. Satisfied with his slaughter, he lifted the saw and turned around to face the last two with a devilish smile on his face.

"You may have broken the entrapment but you still have to get past me," The Stranger said and began to walk over to Kevin while firing the motor of the chainsaw to frighten him some more.

Kevin tried to get up so he could run but his leg was badly sprained and he could barely stand. He picked himself up by holding on to the bottom railings of the stairs and limped as fast as he could but he wasn't fast enough. The Stranger was right behind and was about to raise his saw so he could rip Kevin in half as well.

"Martin!" Andy yelled his name from the fireplace, "Stay away from my brother," She threatened him with the spell book that she held right over the flames in the fireplace.

"I know how important this book is to you. Stay away from my brother or I'll throw it into the fire," She threatened.

The Stranger could tell that she was serious and he didn't want her to destroy the spell book so he took a step and backed away from Kevin.

"Kevin, walk out the door now," Andy said to him.

"What?" Kevin didn't understand.

"Leave Kevin, get out of this house. Go home, find Mom and get her to call the police," She said.

"I can't leave you in here. He'll kill you," Kevin said.

"Maybe he will but at least, you'll make it. One of us has to," She said in tears, "Run now!"

Kevin didn't want to leave her alone but he knew he had to. This was the only chance they had for one of them to survive and who knows? Maybe he'd bring back help before the Stranger is able to kill his sister.

"I'll be back for you," He said and tried to walk past the Stranger but he blocked his path with his chainsaw and fired the motor again.

"You're not going anywhere, Baker,"

"I'm not bluffing, Martin. I know this book is the only chance you have to still exist in this world now that the medallion is destroyed. Let him go or I'll toss it in the fire," She brought the book even closer to the flames.

"You seem to have forgotten that this house operates because of my magic. How can you

burn the book without any fire?" He asked and looked over at the fireplace.

The flames immediately went out and the logs became as cold as ice. Andy was terrified because she had just lost the only leverage she had.

"Now, what will you do?" He mocked her and revved the chainsaw again.

Kevin used his eyes to communicate with his sister. He looked down at his feet and she did the same as well. He was trying to show her that the gasoline can that she had dropped was right by his foot and he was going to kick it to her. She got the message and dipped her hands into her pocket so she could take out the matches.

"Now, where was I?" The Stranger said and turned his attention back on Kevin.

Andy placed the book on the floor and whipped out the matches and Kevin kicked the can over to her. She grabbed it and quickly opened the lid and doused the book with the flammable liquid. She took out a stick of matches and scratched it against the box.

"Stop that!"

The Stranger ran over to her with his chainsaw but before he could get to her, she dropped the lit match onto the book and it caught on fire.

"No…" Martin yelled.

As the spell book caught on fire, so did the Stranger. He was enveloped in flames and he screamed as he got burned all over. Andy ran over to the other side and grabbed Kevin's hand. They backed away from the screaming Stranger and watched him as his dead skin roasted. He fell to his knees, unable to bear the pain of the flames and he fell to the floor, completely still.

The house became quiet again and the Stranger's body was letting out a lot of smoke after the fire around him finally went out.

"Did we do it? Is he dead?" Kevin asked.

Andy slowly walked over to his body and kicked it but nothing happened, just as she'd hoped.

"He's dead. We did it," She ran back to her brother and embraced him, "Come on, let's go home," she said.

They walked across the floor and when they reached Brandon's body, Kevin took one last glance at him before tearing his eyes away. He was in front of Andy so he stepped outside the house first and when he stood on the porch, he looked across the street and saw their house brightly lit up and he noticed someone moving inside through the windows.

"Mom," He said with a sad smile, "Andy, there's mom," He told his sister and when he turned to look at her, he saw that she was still at the edge of the door and hadn't stepped outside yet.

"Andy, are you okay?" He asked.

"I can't—I can't move. I can't move, Kevin," She cried out to him.

"What? Why?" He asked and just as he was about to walk back to her, he noticed the Stranger standing behind her, roasted like a burnt turkey but still alive.

He was the reason Andy couldn't move. He had a hand out facing her and it seemed like he had her in some sort of telekinetic hold and was slowly pulling her further away from the door.

"No, Andy…" Kevin screamed and grabbed his sister's hand, "Hold on, I got you," He assured her and tried to pull her out the door but he couldn't, the Stranger's magical hold on her was too strong.

"Don't let me go, Kevin," Andy begged him in fear, tears pouring out of her eyes.

"I won't, I won't," Kevin told her but her hand was starting to slip out of his.

"I told you that you were not going anywhere. I will not be denied my vengeance," The Stranger yelled.

He pulled even harder at Andy and she slipped out of her brother's hold. She floated through the air and landed right into his hand. Martin held her by the neck and he had her suspended from the floor so she was being choked by his grip.

"Let her go," Kevin screamed and was about to run back inside but he hesitated to.

"Come on now, Kevin. Are you really going to run away and leave your sister to die at my hands?" He asked, trying to manipulate him into coming back inside.

"Even if I come back inside, you're still going to kill her," Kevin cried out.

"That is true, but what kind of a brother would abandon his sister to die mere seconds

after she was willing to sacrifice her life for his?"

Kevin didn't know what to do. Andy was being choked and her eyes were staring to roll to the back of her head. He couldn't leave her to die, he just couldn't. He slowly walked back into the house and stood by the door.

"That's good, Kevin. You are a good brother. Now, close the door,"

Kevin turned around and just as he was closing the door, he looked over at his house again. Home was so close and yet so unreachable. He closed the door and when he turned back around, the Stranger had his hook to Andy's neck.

"Now, that you've decided to stay with us, you can watch your sister die,"

"I—love y-you, K-Kevin," Andy whispered with her last breath.

The Stranger ran his hook into one end of her neck and cut all the way through to the other end before snapping her neck apart. Her body fell to the floor while her head remained in his hand.

"No," Kevin broke down and fell to his knees. Andy's voice saying **I Love You** still echoed in his head because it was the first time she had ever said those three words to him; the first and the last.

The Stranger threw her head over to him and it rolled until it bumped into his legs. Martin looked down at Kevin and could see that the little boy had no fight left in him. The door was right behind him but he didn't even have the will to open it because of how broken he was. He decided to take his time with his final kill so he transformed into his normal form and walked over to a sobbing Kevin.

He knelt down beside him and placed his hand on Kevin's head and patted him gently.

"I know that it hurts, little one. I felt the exact same way you're feeling right now when someone I loved was taken away from me. I felt the same emptiness you feel, the same anger, the same hate and even as I suffocated to death in that grave, I could only think about one thing; destroying the people that had hurt me," Martin told him.

"How did you even survive? We destroyed the medallion and the book," Kevin asked.

"You clearly didn't get all the necessary information. Destroying the medallion only made the house escapable and destroying the spell book was never going to kill me, child. I'm already dead but I was brought back by the hands of a demon and the flames of vengeance. I cannot be killed until my vengeance is complete,"

Kevin suddenly realized something from all that Martin had just said to him. He was brought back to life by a **demon** which was why he was so hard to kill. Kevin remembered that when they were trying to translate the spell book, they came across a page that had a picture of those two daggers in it and when Andy had read that page, she said that the daggers were powerful weapons that could kill a demon on earth. That was what could kill Martin!

Why didn't he realize this sooner? He wondered to himself. That was why when he had stabbed the Stranger before, he seemed hurt and afraid and he ran for his life.

Martin had his eyes on Kevin's face and didn't notice that the kid was slowly pulling the dagger out from within his shirt. Kevin raised his head and looked at Martin straight in the eyes that were reddened with anger.

"So much hate in your eyes, Baker. The same look that your great-grandfather had when he killed my family and had me buried alive," Martin said.

Suddenly, he heard the sound of his flesh tear and his eyes widened in shock, disbelief and pain. Martin looked down at his chest and saw that he had been stabbed with one of the daggers by Kevin and it was right in his heart. He angrily wrapped his hand around Kevin's neck and it made his drive the dagger even deeper into Martin's heart and all the while this happened, their eyes were still locked on each other.

"Nicely done, kid," Martin admired his fighting spirit.

His grip on Kevin's neck loosened and he fell to the floor with a hand on his chest. He was wheezing heavily and his skin began to burn up until he slowly turned to ash and withered away.

Kevin was in tears as he couldn't believe that he had done it. He had survived the stranger's house although it was at a cost but at least, he made it and would be able to tell his story to give Brandon's and Jamie's parents some closure about the deaths of their children.

He dropped the dagger on the floor, got up on his feet and looked at the insides of the house one last time before backing out and running away in tears. He ran back home and when he reached his house, he opened the door and went inside happily.

"Mom! Mom, I'm home. Mom," He called out but no one answered immediately.

The house seemed empty and he didn't understand why. Was she not at home?

"Mom?" He called again and climbed up the stairs to look for her in her room.

He got to her room and opened the door, there was no one inside. Then, he heard those same loud footsteps and clicking sounds that he had heard when he was still at the Stranger's house. He couldn't be hearing those sounds because Martin was dead, right? His heart was beating faster and sweat was dripping from his forehead. He stepped out of his mom's room and slowly walked over to the edge of the staircase and he saw the Stranger standing right at the mouth of the door downstairs with his hook in his hand.

"No, you can't be here. I killed you. I stabbed you with the dagger," Kevin said to him from upstairs, shaking his head in disbelief.

"You stabbed me with one of the daggers," The Stranger said and held out both daggers in his hands while moving closer to the stairs, ***"The twin***

daggers of Orishirishi were made as a working pair. The power to kill a demon is too much to be contained in just one physical object so the creators of these weapon made two of them and they have to be used at the same time,"

"But, how are you in my house? You can't leave your house without the medallion," Kevin asked.

"You mean this medallion?" The Stranger asked and was now behind Kevin up on the stairs. The medallion was completely restored in his hands and didn't have a scratch on it.

Kevin flinched in fright as Martin appeared beside him so tripped and fell down the stairs. After he landed at the bottom of the stairs, he grunted and tried to get up but he was too hurt.

"Your sister didn't read the entire page about breaking the entrapment spell, did she?" Martin appeared right beside Kevin on the floor and loomed over him, *"Let me finish it for you; To end the spell and free the entrapped, the medallion of Moriah would have to be destroyed and melted in fire but you kids only destroyed it,"*

"So that means…" Kevin said.

"You never left my house,"

The entire interior of the house rippled and separated apart and transformed back into the Stranger's house, just as it was before he left.

"This is your new home now," The Stranger said and pulled out his large hook.

"No," Kevin panicked and scrambled up to his

feet.

He ran for the open door but before he got to it, it slammed shut and locked him in. He banged on the door several times, trying to get out as the Stranger approached him to finish him off.

He screamed as he realized that his time was up and the echoes of his panicked cries filled the air until they withered away into a voiceless shriek.

END

EPILOGUE

The police cars had all come and left after Jolene and Joseph called them in to officially report their children as 'Missing'. After taking their descriptions and filling the report, the cops left the divorced couple alone while they conducted their search.

Jolene was very unsettled about her missing children and Joseph did everything he could to make light of the situation and make her as comfortable as possible. He ordered them some dinner and although she didn't have an appetite, he got her to eat a little bit. It took a while for her to fall asleep but after patting her head and singing to her for a few hours, she finally dozed off and so did he.

Later in the middle of the night, Joseph opened his eyes and looked over at Jolene. She looked so tired and uncomfortable so he decided to take her up to her bed. He carried her in his arms, took her upstairs to her bedroom and tucked her in.

"I promise you that I won't rest until I bring our kids back home to you," He whispered to her and kissed her forehead before walking away.

He went back downstairs and walked into the kitchen to get a drink. He took a cup and opened the tap. He put the glass in his mouth and just as he was about to drink, he looked toward one of the open windows and noticed that there was a lot of light coming from the house just opposite.

He walked over to the window to inspect and when he looked outside, he could see that almost all the lights of the house were turned on. He kept looking and then, he noticed someone standing by one of the windows of the house and he was 100% certain that it was his son.

 "Kevin?" He asked himself and his glass of water slipped out of his hand, forcing him to look away.

When he looked back outside, there was no one standing by the window. He knew that he didn't just imagine what he saw so he decided to go and check it out.

He put on a jacket and walked out of the house. He crossed the street and went to the opposite house. He stepped onto the porch and knocked on the door.

Just as he did, the door creaked wide open on its own, "Hello, is anyone here?" Joseph asked but he didn't get any response.

 He stepped inside the house and kept calling out to

anyone but there was no answer.

The lights in the house began to flicker until most of them went out. Just after that, Joseph heard some footsteps coming from upstairs so he looked up to see who it was and much to his surprise, it was Andy and she walked from one end of the corridor to the other.

"Andy?" He called her but she didn't stop until she was out of sight.

"Andy?" He called again and ran up the stairs to get her.

He reached up and looked in the direction she had walked in but she was gone. He saw a door right there and he slowly approached it. He opened the door and stepped inside the room and was greeted with the terrible sight of his children's bloody, disfigured, dead and dismembered bodies hanging on the wall along with a bunch of skeletons.

"No, no, it can't be," He cried out in a horrified panic.

He suddenly felt someone behind him and when he turned around, he saw the Stranger with his hook in his hand.

"Every child will be taken and that includes

you, Baker,"

The Stranger ran his hook right through Joseph's head and killed him instantly. He had a smile on his face and a look in his eyes that surely meant that he was just getting started and that he had many more victims left to get his revenge on

ABOUT THE AUTHOR

Otis Obarakpor Bright, Pen-name Otis Bright, is a Nigerian author, poet, scriptwriter and novelist. He is a young recognized author who has already published multiple E-Novels on many online platforms like Light Reader, Good Novel, Web Novel and so many more.

He is known for his imaginativeness, humor, dark action-packed style and expert technique for writing all genres but mostly supernatural stories with spine-tingling action and unfathomable suspense. His novels are rated highly in Nigeria and he has some readers all over the world who hold his works in high esteem.